THE
WILD CATS
OF
ROME

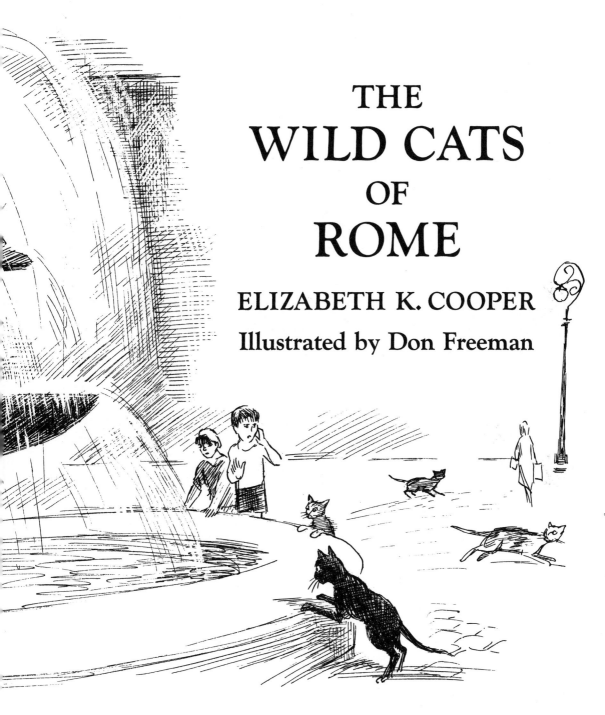

THE
WILD CATS
OF
ROME

ELIZABETH K. COOPER

Illustrated by Don Freeman

GOLDEN GATE JUNIOR BOOKS
San Carlos • California

CONTENTS

THE GREAT BLACK CAT

THE CITY OF Rome has hundreds of fountains, thousands of cats, and millions of people. The fountains belong to the people and the cats belong to themselves. They are born in the rubble of ancient buildings. They grow up and run wild through the old city, uncared for, unwanted, and unloved.

The wild cats race through the narrow streets and dark alleys that thread through the city. They hide quickly in time of danger and reappear just as quickly when the danger is over. On a day that seems catless they are resting in churches, watching from behind statues, napping in shadowy

7

doorways, or hiding under parked cars from the dogs in the streets. In Rome the wild cats are always there. They have been there for many hundreds of years.

Night after night the cats prowl the back alleys, hunting for scraps and fighting among themselves over garbage. The good prowlers, hunters, and fighters find plenty to eat. The weak, timid ones live always with hunger.

All the wild cats suffer from thirst, especially on warm days. Panting with parched tongues, they are drawn to the Roman fountains, where they spring up silently to the rims for a few laps of fresh water and a few drops of cooling spray. But the people who crowd around the fountains do not welcome the cats.

"Get away! Scat!" cry the tourists.

"*Va via, subito!*" cry the Romans.

The cats race off in all directions, but they always return to try again to sip clean water from a fountain. When this is not possible, they must lap up the dark, oily water that runs in street gutters, or lick dirty sidewalks wherever small puddles have formed.

On the very first hot day of the year, Angelo, the great black cat, slipped out of the church where he had found shelter from the fierce rays of the midday sun. He made his way through the traffic of late afternoon. Everywhere crowds were hurrying home from work. As he dashed across the streets, cars honked, motorcycles roared, and men shook their fists and shouted at him in anger. Angelo knew that he should have stayed longer in the cool, quiet church, but his throat was hot and dry and his coat was powdered with the dust of the busy streets. Parched and discouraged, he thought of the heat of the summer yet to come. He must have water! He began to run.

As he ran he glanced back over his shoulder and saw that he was followed by a long and motley procession of cats. There were big cats and small ones, young cats with agile gait, and elderly cats barely able to limp along. Angelo knew that all of them were thirsty and expecting him to lead them to water. This was nothing new or unusual for Angelo, for he was the leader of the wild cats of Rome.

Angelo had been destined for leadership ever since that moonlit night when, as a tiny kitten, he had left the warmth and security of his mother and had struck out for himself. From then on he had found his own food, slept in his private place behind some rubbish cans in an alley, washed his own face, and brushed his own whiskers. By the time he was fully grown he was unusually large, unusually black and shining, and he held his head unusually high when he walked.

He preferred to walk alone. Soon, however, other cats began to follow him, though usually at a respectful distance. There was nothing modest about the great black cat. How could there be? He knew that he was the biggest, the blackest, the handsomest cat in all Rome. He knew that the other cats were his followers whether he wished it or not. However, he had an uneasy feeling that leadership would, sooner or later, place responsibilities on his shoulders.

It was his leadership position that had caused him to seek a name for himself. In his wanderings through the city Angelo had heard tales of great Roman leaders. "Every one of them had a name," said the cat to himself. "I too must have a name, a special name, one that is right for me."

The cat knew he would find his name somewhere in Rome. "I'll recognize it as soon as I hear it," he decided as he set out to prowl through the city he loved.

He found his name in a vast, shadowy church in front of the gigantic marble statue of Moses. He was gazing upward at the powerful leg, the sinewy knee, the strong hands, the noble head when his sharp ears picked up words that he understood.

"This magnificent sculpture is the work of Michaelangelo," said a man who was lecturing to a group of tourists gathered around the statue. "Michaelangelo is probably the greatest artist who ever lived."

The voice went on, but the cat no longer listened. He knew he had found his name.

"*Michael*-Angelo, Michael-*Angelo*," he purred over and over. And then, "Angelo, The Cat. Angelo, The Great Black Cat. Angelo, Wild Cat of Rome. Angelo! ANGELO!" That

was it! In this moment he felt more intensely than ever before that he belonged to Rome and that Rome belonged to him.

Now Angelo ran on, down one street after another, dodging in and out among the honking cars, the crowds of people.

Suddenly, there it was, a small fountain in the center of a small piazza. Angelo leaped gracefully to the rim of the little pool and was about to lower his head to drink when some women with loud voices and many bundles pushed him away from the water and then used their feet to shoo him across the hot cobblestones.

Waves of heat rose from the stones as Angelo paused to catch his breath. He tried to clean his dusty coat, but as he licked his fur his tongue became coated with grime. He looked back at the fountain and longed to approach it, to wash off his tongue, to fill his parched mouth with cool water and feel it trickling down his burning throat. But as soon as he made any move toward the pool the women threatened him anew and drove him back.

Angelo finally turned and ran, though not with his usual speed. After him ran his thirsty followers. This time, Angelo led them to a piazza which was walled in by handsome old buildings. Against one of the buildings stood the great Fountain of Trevi. As parched as he was, Angelo stood for a moment admiring the columns and statues and waterfalls. Best of all, for his purpose, was the wide shallow pool where a hot, thirsty cat, with luck, might lap up a drink.

By now the afternoon was ending and only a few tourists stood at the edge of the pool, making wishes and tossing in coins. Behind the tourists barefoot boys waited for them to move on. Then they would wade into the pond after the silver and copper coins that lay on the bottom.

Angelo crept up to the edge, choosing his spot carefully. It was away from the few tourists who remained, and away from the boys, who watched and waited. He sprang to the rim and dipped his dry tongue into the water.

A boy jumped fast. *"Un gatto! Subito!"* he cried as he pushed Angelo off the rim into the water. The pool was shallow, but deep enough to drown a cat. Angelo sank, rose sputtering to the top, then sank again. But the next time he came up he somehow managed to scramble to the edge, pull himself up to the rim, and then spring down and escape the laughing boys. Angelo's followers had run off, spreading out in all directions, each heading for his own hiding place somewhere in the city.

Angelo did not run or slink away. For him, the ducking in the pool had been an indignity, but he held his head as erect as ever as he marched across the piazza, water dripping from his coat. At least he had had a drink, and his tongue was again pink and rough, his fur no longer covered with dust.

But Angelo was far from satisfied. He was a leader who had failed his followers. Nowhere in the city could he find a place where cats could refresh themselves on a hot day. It was a problem that troubled his mind.

He made his way to a quiet spot among the fallen stones of the ancient Colosseum. Here Angelo had a secret place where he sometimes came to think and be alone. His hiding place was barely reached by the slanting rays of the setting sun as he sat and groomed himself, from his elegant whiskers to his silky tail.

"Perhaps I too would lick water from the streets as the others

do if I did not love the fountains," he mused to himself as the sun went down. "In a city of fountains, is there not one, somewhere. . .?"

Then it struck him—a big idea, a great plan. It was so big and great that he was almost afraid to put it into words, even to himself.

"What this city needs," he purred very softly, "is a fountain for cats! A fountain for cats only! I will see that such a fountain is built."

With that, Angelo's life work began.

ANGELO'S QUEST

Along the narrow winding streets of Rome are many studios where artists work with stone. Angelo, who knew his way through the city, went from place to place looking for someone who made fountains. In his mind he pictured his fountain for cats. It need not be, he thought, as big or as grand as the Fountain of Trevi. But it must be beautiful, with a low pool that a cat could reach safely, and some handsome sculpture from which cool water would gush and flow.

He wondered, was Michaelangelo still making statues? If not, he would find someone else. Surely, he thought, someone in Rome must make figures for fountains.

He walked until the pads of his paws were raw and burning from the pavements. He looked and listened and searched, but without success.

He found one yard where men chipped and chiseled rock into angels as big as giants. But the stone figures were for graves, not for fountains.

He found a place where small clay figures were modeled and glazed and baked hard in ovens. He found a big workshop where girls made ghostly little white plaster copies of the great statue of Moses.

He found a modern studio, too, and there he watched the young artists bending steel rods and welding them to make strange, airy forms. "Interesting," Angelo said to himself. "I wonder how something like that would look on my fountain."

In the days of his quest Angelo ate very little. When he was too weary to go on, he refreshed himself with cat naps. He was often discouraged but he never gave up. Walking alone, he combed the streets of Rome. He found where statues were made for parks and gardens and for the altars of churches. He found workmen who patched up ancient statues that had lost a nose, an arm, or some fingers, but no one at all who made fountains. Men worked on bird baths and on fonts for holy water, but no one, it seemed, any longer worked on fountains.

On one of his prowls Angelo came to a shabby little building on a dead-end street. On a high old wall that enclosed the courtyard was a sign so weather-worn that its words could hardly be seen. Slowly, letter by letter, his heart pounding with hope, Angelo read the sign.

FABRICA Di FONTANE

It was a fountain factory!

"At last! cried Angelo. "My search is over!"

He pushed open the old gate, walked across the shabby courtyard, and entered the *fabrica*. He was in a shop where a young man was hammering at a bench that was littered with pipes. Another man, small and bent, sat in a dark corner of the shop and stared into space. The only sound was the clang of the hammer on the pipe.

For a moment Angelo had doubts. Had the sign been wrong? Was it, perhaps, an old one left over from the past? Then he looked around the room and saw the yellowed pictures that lined the walls. Faded as they now were, they were pictures of fountains—small ones and big ones, many of them with beautiful statues.

Filled with joy, Angelo took a long leap and sprang onto the workbench. He stood on the tools and pipes and addressed the workman in a loud and persuasive voice.

"I have searched the whole city, and at last I have found you," he cried. "O maker of fountains, you will build the fountain we need, the fountain for the thirsty wild cats of Rome!"

"Get this howling cat out of here, Nonno!" shouted the young worker as he pushed Angelo off the workbench. "In this city the cats are nearly as bad as the rats!"

The small bent man rose slowly from his stool and led the way to the courtyard. "*Vieni, povero gatto*," he said as he limped along.

"Poor cat, indeed! How dare they speak so to me!" thought Angelo as he walked out with his head held high. Still, he was shaken, and he paused in the dusty courtyard to smooth his fur and calm his spirit. Somehow he had never expected to be turned down. It was as though the man in the shop had not heard a word he had spoken.

Angelo began to think deeply about people, those big two-legged animals who had taken over the streets and buildings of Rome. Until now they had not mattered to Angelo, except as nuisances to be endured. But suddenly, for the first time in his independent young life, Angelo needed human assistance. But how could he get them to listen?

"My followers understand what I say," Angelo said to himself. "Can it be that *people* do not understand me when I speak? Strange, for I can understand them."

Angelo had almost, but not quite, decided to accept the hopelessness of trying to communicate with human beings when the small bent man came limping out into the court-yard. He hobbled over to Angelo, murmuring softly as he came. In his hands he had a slab of black bread and a bowl of milk. He placed the milk on the cobblestones and said with a kind of bow, "Please drink, good cat."

Angelo appreciated the polite words and was quite amazed at the invitation. Nothing like this had ever happened to him before.

"Thank you," he purred and then bent over the bowl and began lapping up the milk. How sweet, how fresh, how wonderful! He had all but forgotten the delicious taste of milk. Since that long-ago night when he had left his mother, he had tasted milk only two or three times. Like other wild cats, his only milk was lapped from a sidewalk or street after someone had carelessly dropped a bottle. How different, he thought, to drink milk like this, from a deep, clean bowl, with none of the dust and grime of the street!

When the bowl was empty, he studied the small man, whose back was strangely bent and whose legs were strangely twisted and thin. "I wish I could thank him," said Angelo aloud. "If only he could understand what I say."

"But I do understand you, good cat," said the man. "And I understood you when you spoke in the workshop about the fountain you want for the wild cats of Rome."

"Then people can understand cats!" cried Angelo.

"No, they can't," said the man, shaking his head sadly. "But I am different. I understand what you say and I understand what you feel. When I was young I too longed to build something great, something lasting. I can't remember what it was that I wanted to build. . ." His voice seemed to fade away.

"Was it a statue? Or a bridge across the Tiber, a bridge with statues on it? Or perhaps a fountain with statues in the middle?" asked Angelo eagerly.

"I don't know," said the man. "All I remember is that I was working on something big—and some ropes broke, and a piece of marble fell, and I was under the marble. Since then I forget many things, and I talk to cats."

"But that is good," said Angelo.

"No, that is bad," said the man. "It is bad for me. People make fun of me and say that I'm queer in the head."

"Do you work here? Or do you live here?" asked Angelo.

"Both," said the man. "I help Tonio when he needs me, and I clean up the workshop when he goes home for the night. He gives me my milk and bread and cheese and a cot to sleep on at night."

"Then we can work here together!" cried Angelo, more excited than he had been in weeks.

"Work? Work?" The man seemed puzzled.

"Yes, work," said Angelo. "I can tell by your eyes, your face, your hands that you are an artist."

"An artist," said the man, looking more puzzled than before.

"Yes, an artist! I need you and you need me. I have searched all over Rome for a man like you." As Angelo spoke his eloquence increased, for he had caught sight of a number of his followers who had gathered silently and were now seated on top of the courtyard wall.

"Courage, my friend!" cried Angelo to the bent little man. "Never despair. I will return tonight when you are alone. Then we shall plan the building of our fountain!"

The man rubbed his head and watched as the great black cat made a graceful dash up the trunk of a tree, leaped across to the wall, and disappeared on the other side.

For a full minute all was still. Neither sound nor motion disturbed the midday air. Then, "Hooray for Angelo!" rang out from the cats on the wall as they followed their leader.

"Hooray for Angelo," whispered the man as he shrugged his twisted shoulders. He stared for awhile at the courtyard wall and then limped slowly back into the workshop.

NONNO AND ANGELO

When the first breezes of evening were cooling the courtyard of the Fabrica Di Fontane Angelo returned. The bent little man was sitting on the workshop steps finishing his supper of bread and cheese.

"Are you alone?" Angelo asked.

"Alone and free," said the man. "Tonio went home for the night. I have swept the floor and put away all the tools. Here, I saved some of my supper for you." He put down some pieces of cheese.

"Thank you," said Angelo, "but I did not come here to

27

eat. I came to talk about fountains, Signore . . . Signore what? I don't know your name."

"I don't either!" cried the man, laughing loudly as though at a joke. "I don't know my first name or my last. Tonio calls me Nonno, but I'm sure I'm not his grandfather. I don't think I'm anybody's grandfather, but they all call me Nonno."

"Then I will call you the same, Signore Nonno," said Angelo politely.

"Plain Nonno will do," said the man as he nodded and shrugged his shoulders. Then he squinted his small bright eyes and studied the top of the courtyard wall. There, one by one in orderly rows, the wild cats had begun to assemble in silence.

"Look, so many cats!" cried Nonno.

"They are some of my followers," explained Angelo with pride. "No one looks after them, and they are thirsty most of the time. It is for them that the fountain must be built."

"*Buona sera*," said Nonno to the cats on the wall. "*Buona sera*," he said to the ones he had spotted in the dusty old plane tree.

"*Buona sera*," answered all the wild cats together. The sound of their many voices traveled up to the very tops of the nearby buildings. Children in bed stirred in their sleep. Grownups leaned from their windows and cried out against the howling of the wild cats in the courtyard below.

But Nonno bowed politely to the cats and told them to make themselves comfortable while he and Angelo talked about fountains.

Angelo explained in detail what he wanted—a new fountain, a special fountain, a fountain just for cats.

"It must be beautiful," he said, "like the other fountains of Rome. It must have jets of water that make mist to hold rainbows in the sunlight. Around it must be a shallow pool, with a wide rim where cats can sit safely and drink, and where they can cool their hot, dusty paws in the water."

"*Si! Si!*" said Nonno, nodding as though a full-color picture of Angelo's fountain were developing inside his head.

Angelo continued, "And the fountain must have something high like a statue in the middle where the water shoots up. People will have to stand back and not drive us away. The fountain will be ours, for cats only!"

As Angelo paused to catch his breath, Nonno began to rock back and forth and speak to himself, making soft moaning sounds. "Ah me, ah me," he moaned. "Have I any marble? No. Have I any granite? No. Have I rock of any kind? No."

"Then what will you use for our fountain?" Angelo asked, aware that the silent cats around him were listening intently.

"Nothing," answered Nonno. "I have nothing but the clothes on my back and an old sack that I carry when I walk at night in the streets."

A heavy stillness fell on the courtyard. Nothing moved, not even a whisker or tail.

"But I can buy the things that we need," said Nonno. "Just give me the money and I will build you a fountain."

"Money!" cried Angelo with disdain. "Cats have no money. We cats need no money."

"Well, then," said Nonno, "no money, no fountain. That is the way of the world." He rose awkwardly to his feet, hobbled across the uneven cobblestones, and disappeared through the workshop door.

"*Buona notte*," Angelo called after him, but there was no answering good night from Nonno.

Angelo went over to the step and called through the open door, "Now hear me, Nonno! I will be back!" The great black cat turned to speak to his followers, but the top of the wall was bare. His followers had disappeared into the night.

Fighting back his deep sense of failure, Angelo departed as he had arrived. With his head held high, he walked alone through the courtyard gate. He did not blame his followers for having deserted him. He was the leader, but where had he led them? He had given them hope, and their hope was now dead. He had made sparkling promises that he was not able to keep.

Yet, as low as Angelo felt at the moment, his despair

was not absolute. Down deep in his skull, his complicated cat brain was ticking away, discarding old ideas and constructing new ones. What he needed now, he decided, was a little time—to rest, to sleep, and to dream.

In the deepening shadows of night, he found his way to the ancient Colosseum. There, as the moon sailed out from behind a cloud, he climbed up and up and finally stretched out on one of the centuries-old stones near the top. He tried to think, to make plans, but the harder he tried, the more weary he grew. As a ray of moonlight fell across his relaxed form he yawned several times and fell into a deep sleep.

ANGELO'S PLAN

Iт was broad daylight when Angelo wakened to the noisy chirping of two small birds who were building a nest in a sheltered corner above his head. He was hungry, but the birds were small ones. He knew from past experience that they were mainly feathers and bones, with not enough meat to make them worth the trouble of catching.

He stared up at the partly finished nest and watched lazily as the little birds flew to and fro. Each time one returned to the nest it brought from somewhere a bit of twig, some string, a shred of cloth or paper, ravels of wool, tufts of grass, or a sliver of foil that glinted in the light. How neatly and cleverly the nest was made, thought Angelo. How well the birds built, using only the odds and ends they had picked up in their flights through the city.

Angelo jumped as his mind was suddenly illuminated by a burst of ideas. "That's it! *That's it!*" he cried in a mighty meow. "If the wild birds of Rome can do it, so can we!"

He knew now how to build the fountain.

At Angelo's burst of exuberance, the little birds huddled in a corner in fright. But the great black cat was leaping down to the Colosseum exit, headed for a meeting with Nonno in the courtyard of the Fabrica Di Fontane.

On his way he passed a small white cat in the street. "Go quickly," he said to her urgently. "Tell the others that we meet tonight in the courtyard. Tonight we shall plan for our fountain. You will all be needed."

The cat raced off to pass the good word to the other followers as Angelo sped on to the courtyard. All the rest of the day he waited there on a branch of the plane tree until Tonio had left for the night. He watched as Nonno swept the day's litter out the door and onto the old cobblestones. Then, as soon as Nonno had settled on the steps to eat his supper, Angelo sprang down and faced him.

"I said I'd be back and here I am," said Angelo.

"You have brought money?" Nonno asked.

"I have something better than money," declared Angelo.

"I have a plan."

"A plan." Nonno turned his head away and spat on the cobblestones to show what he thought of plans.

"Angelo always has plans," meowed a large yellow cat who had just seated himself on top of the courtyard wall.

"Yes, Angelo and his big plans," said another cat with a meow that sounded very much like a laugh.

The followers were gathering now—on top of the wall, on the branches of the dusty tree, and on the cobblestones of the yard. Most of them stayed just beyond the full glow of the street lamp, for they felt freer to speak when they were shadowed by darkness. Angelo, however, chose the golden patch of light, and he stood in it as an actor stands in a spotlight.

"It is true," he said in a loud, clear voice, "that I have a plan, and it is indeed a very big plan. The plan is much bigger than I am, and so I need Nonno's help, and—most of all—I need yours! I am just one," Angelo continued, "but you are many. I know just so much, but all of us together —think what we know!"

"Do we know how to make a fountain?" the yellow cat called out.

"No money, no fountain," muttered Nonno. "No money, no fountain."

"Wait! Wait!" cried Angelo. "We cats have never had money, but we have always survived. No one in Rome has ever looked after us. But we can take care of ourselves! We have our ways *and we never give up!*"

By now the wild cats were listening intently. "Bravo! That is very true!" one of them sang out and others lifted their heads in a mighty meow.

Angelo went on. "Do not worry about materials for our fountain. Rome is filled with materials, just lying around ready to be picked up and used. We cats know the streets and the back alleys, the rubbish cans and the dumps. We

will find everything we need for our fountain. We shall find what is needed, and Nonno, with his sack, will bring the things here. Our motto is, *'We find what we need and we use what we find.'* Now, let us all go and search through the city!"

With that, Angelo said his goodnight to Nonno. Then he turned and marched sedately out through the courtyard gate.

One by one and two by two, the rest of the wild cats followed, moving softly on padded paws.

"WE FIND
WHAT WE NEED..."

Fʀᴏᴍ ᴛʜᴇɴ ᴏɴ, night and day, the wild cats were seen
more than ever prowling over Rome. They traveled in bands
of a dozen or more, roaming the streets and alleys and
pawing through the rubbish heaps of the city.

Angelo seemed to be everywhere at once. He led groups,
found new paths through the dark forgotten passageways
of old Rome, and pointed out treasures that Nonno might
use in building the fountain.

As he went along he kept calling out to his followers,
"Remember our ancient motto, 'We find what we need

and we use what we find.' " Angelo knew, of course, that he himself had made up the "ancient motto" right after he had seen the birds building their nest. But by now he had repeated the words so often that even to him *We find what we need, and we use what we find*" seemed to be the key to the survival of cats through the many downfalls of Rome. Ancient or not, the motto inspired Angelo's followers as they roamed the city, hunting silently for materials for Nonno to pick up and carry home in his old sack.

Some of the cats kept special watch over the little sidewalk cafés where people sat at small tables for hours and poured wine from bright bottles. Sometimes a careless drinker would tip over his bottle, to send it crashing to the pavement, scattering bits of jewel-colored glass—golden amber, ruby red, topaz yellow, or emerald green. When the sparkling bits were swept up and dumped into a bin in the alley, the sharp-eyed cats would remember the place and lead Nonno to it after dark.

Some of the cats stationed themselves at hotels, some around espresso bars where people in a hurry dropped in for small cups of coffee. What treasures the cats spotted at such places! Broken cups and saucers, shiny and white as angel wings. Broken plates, some with gold rims and some with pictures of fruits and flowers. Broken earthenware bowls thickly glazed in green or blue or brown.

On a night when one of Angelo's assistants was searching

the courtyard of an especially elegant building, he found a cracked ash tray with VIVA ROMA in red and green. Later, in the garden of the same building, he unearthed an old cream pitcher. The handle was missing and the bowl was cracked, but it was covered with real gold.

Day after day and night after night Angelo and his followers discovered more treasure than Nonno could possibly carry in his worn old sack. He rummaged through the junk that had been gathering for years in the courtyard of the Fabrica Di Fontane and at last found just what he needed. It was a broken-down pushcart that had been discarded and forgotten long ago. Nonno worked on it for a few evenings, patching up the hole in one side, replacing the wheel that had fallen off, and then brushing it all with his broom to make it ready for its cargo of treasure.

While Nonno was busy fixing up the two-wheeled cart, Angelo made his most important find. He led a band of his hardiest followers to the edge of the city where a new apartment house was being built. The workmen had gone home for the day, leaving their ladders for the cats to climb as they inspected the structure from cellar to roof. Everywhere Angelo looked he saw floors littered with things that could be used in making the fountain. Bits of shiny copper wire left over from the electrical work. Broken blue tiles from the kitchen walls and counters. Yellow and green tiles from the bathrooms and halls. Bent hinges, iron bolts, empty paint cans, and large chips of painted plaster. They were all lying there, waiting to be taken. Best of all were the many little heaps of sand and cement and the discarded cement bags that could easily be filled.

Angelo knew that as soon as these things were safely in Nonno's courtyard work on the fountain could begin. His only worry was that the bent little man might not be able to climb the ladders and carry down the materials. He need not have worried, for Nonno, with help and encouragement from Angelo and his followers, worked his way up the tall ladders rung by rung. A coil of heavy rope hung over his right shoulder and under his left arm. "I found this in the workshop," he explained to Angelo. "For tonight's work I have borrowed it. Just for tonight."

Nonno and the cats gathered their treasures together on each of the floors and packed them in old paint cans and dusty bags. Then, one floor at a time, Nonno lowered the bags and cans to the ground where he had left his pushcart.

It was a long, hard haul back to the Fabrica Di Fontane. Twice on the way Nonno had been ready to give up, to abandon his cart and the treasures it held, and to hurry on to his bed and his sleep. But Angelo was always at his side with a word or a song to cheer him.

As the first faint glimmer of day was visible over the tall buildings of the city, Angelo sang out,

"O sole mio,

O fountain spray,

O sparkling fountain,

O happy day!"

Nonno soon joined in and together they sang their way back to the shabby courtyard where they unloaded their materials in a dusty corner behind some tall rubbish cans. There Nonno kept his assortment of bits and pieces, screened from view on one side by the rubbish cans and on the other sides by the workshop wall. It was a good little studio where Nonno and Angelo could work at night, well lit by the street light beyond the wall.

"No more work today," said Angelo as soon as the cart had been emptied. "This is Sunday and we must all rest and sleep. But tonight, my friend, we can begin our great work—building the fountain for the cats of Rome!"

"*Si, si,*" agreed Nonno. "Tonight we begin."

"*Arrivederci,*" called Angelo as he left the courtyard, headed for one of his secret haunts in the city. Walking along the Sunday-quiet streets of Rome, he could not hold back his song of hope and joy. "*O sole mio!*" he sang at the top of his voice. "*O glorious fountain! O happy day!*"

BUILDING THE FOUNTAIN

THAT NIGHT ANGELO and his followers came to the court-yard. There, in a patch of yellow light from the street lamp, work on the fountain began. Nonno, with Angelo as his adviser and helper, marked out an area for the fountain pool. They had already agreed on a suitable location, in a corner where the two walls of the courtyard met.

Nonno surprised himself and delighted Angelo by remembering things he had long forgotten. Somehow, he knew just how to mark out spaces with pegs and string; how to mix sand, cement, and water for concrete; how to make a fine plaster; how to chip a piece of glass or tile to shape it for a special purpose. As he worked he often exclaimed, "See, I remember! I can still do it!"

Then the cats on the wall would lift their heads and cry, "Bravo! Bravo!" People in nearby buildings would lament that the street cats were getting noisier and noisier. But Nonno understood the approving cheers, and he worked harder and better than ever.

Nonno and Angelo worked every night for three or four hours. When Angelo saw Nonno begin to yawn, he would call out, "Enough for tonight. We meet again after sundown tomorrow." Then Nonno would put away the tools he had borrowed from the workshop and go indoors for his sleep. The cats would disappear from the wall as each went its own way in search of food and a safe place to rest. Only Angelo would remain, to watch over the beginnings of the fountain, to embellish his dreams as he pictured in his mind what the finished fountain would be like.

One morning Tonio came to work earlier than usual. Nonno was not on his stool in the dark corner of the workshop and so Tonio went out to look for him. He found him sorting pieces of broken glass in neat piles and talking to Angelo as he worked.

"Get out! Shoo!" shouted Tonio at the cat.

"I was just about to leave," said Angelo with dignity.

Then he leaped to the top of the wall where he flattened himself and kept eyes and ears on what happened below.

"Nonno, don't you remember that I told you to keep that noisy cat away from here?" said Tonio, as though he were speaking to a child.

"Angelo is my friend," Nonno answered with dignity. "We are working together. We are making something important."

Tonio looked around at the heaps of broken bottles, tangled wires, and chipped chinaware. "Making something —out of this junk?" he asked.

"It's not junk!" cried Nonno. "It's treasure. We worked hard to find it and to bring it here."

Tonio was puzzled. "We? Who works here with you?"

"My friend Angelo and the other wild cats. Our motto is —'*We find what we need, and we use what we find!*'" said Nonno slowly and with pride.

"Oh, you do, do you?" Tonio cried as he spotted a sack of cement on the cobblestones. "And just where did you find this good cement? In my workshop, that's where! I pay hard-earned money for my cement, Nonno. I can't afford to have you help yourself."

"No! No!" protested Nonno as Tonio picked up the bag of precious cement and was about to carry it indoors. "I do not take your things! The cement is ours, Angelo's and mine! We scraped it up where the workmen left it, at the edge of the city where new buildings are going up. Please do not take it away from us now."

Tonio opened the bag and let some of the cement run through his fingers. "Yes, I see that it's different from mine. This has some dust and sawdust mixed in. I'm sorry, Nonno," he said as he put down the bag. "You were telling the truth."

"I do not lie and I do not steal," said Nonno solemnly.

"But you do talk to cats, Nonno, and people notice such things. My wife's brother keeps telling me about it. He thinks you should be put away."

"Just because I talk with Angelo and Angelo talks with me? Hah! You tell your wife's brother that Angelo has more sense than he has!"

Tonio laughed. "He may have, at that," he said. "Anyway, I'm not going to have you put away, so don't worry. You can stay here, and you can keep on playing with your bits of junk if it makes you happy."

From then on Tonio stayed away from Nonno's end of the courtyard. During the day Nonno worked indoors. But his real work was done at night, out in the yard with Angelo.

First, Nonno made a large shallow basin, built up of old stones and broken bricks. It was then made smooth and watertight with a thin layer of concrete. Inside the basin, set firmly in the concrete, were pieces of bright tile and colored china.

Next, the outer wall of the low basin was carefully shaped, and its top was flattened to make a place where a cat could sit safely and in comfort.

"Good!" said Angelo. "This pool for our fountain is not too wide and not too deep. But it does look rather plain on the outside."

Nonno smiled his crooked little smile. "Just wait," he said mysteriously. "I first modeled the pool, and now I will make it beautiful."

He sat with his legs outspread and began to select from his well-sorted piles of chipped glass. "Some blue, I think," he said to himself, "and some green for the borders."

As Angelo and his followers watched, Nonno created a mosaic—a delicate picture puzzle formed from hundreds of small bits of glass. From time to time he would ask for help. "Angelo," he would call out, "I need more blue for this flower." Or, "Angelo, do we have any more amber like the bottom of this beer bottle?"

Angelo and some of his helpers would then paw through the heaps of treasure they had collected. If they found what was needed, they would bring it to Nonno or tell him where to pick it up. But if their search proved fruitless, as sometimes happened, all work would stop while Nonno and the cats took to the streets where, sooner or later, they found what they sought. Then they all returned, a triumphant band, and work on the fountain would continue.

In time the entire rim and base of the pool were covered with mosaic pictures in bits of bright colored glass that shone jewel-like in the glow of the street lamp.

"There, that is finished," said Nonno one night as he stood back to survey his work. *"Bella, bella."*

"Yes, it is beautiful—as far as it goes," said Angelo with some anxiety. "But it is only a pool, not a fountain. A fountain goes up. A fountain must have high things in the middle where the water shoots out."

"Of course," Nonno agreed calmly. "I am now ready to build the things that go up." And he began again to work with renewed energy. He worked as one in a dream. He worked without drawings or diagrams. And any plans he may have had were private ones in his own mind.

Night after night Nonno worked. Angelo helped when he could. The other wild cats formed a ring of silent observers, watching, waiting, and dozing on top of the wall and in the old tree.

On most nights the skies were clear, even when summer had ended and the air had begun to grow cold. When storms came and rain beat down in the courtyard, Nonno huddled in the workshop and Angelo found shelter in an overturned box among the rubbish bins. Angelo's followers deserted their observation posts, and they all waited impatiently for the weather to change and the work to go on.

Week followed week and month followed month, through

the autumn, winter, and spring. Bit by bit, step by step, and piece by piece the fountain structure was built.

Rising from the center of the china-studded basin were airy towers with strangely shaped spires fashioned of twisted metal and ornamented with pieces of broken tile and glass. The pieces were set in plaster and cement, each as artfully placed as a precious gem in the crown of a king.

On the rim of the little pool was a kind of throne. The back of the seat was shaped like a shell, with VIVA ROMA across it in letters of red and green. Chips of gold from the cream pitcher had been used in the border that decorated the little throne.

Angelo studied the fountain very early one morning and decided that it was finished at last. "It is perfect!" he said to Nonno. "I can think of nothing to add." He could say no more for his voice was choked with emotion. The strange, jewel-like structure was as beautiful as anything he had ever seen, even in one of his dreams. It was so beautifully Italian, so handsomely Roman, so completely worthy of the wild cats for whom it had been built.

But as Nonno stood back and looked over his work an expression of doubt spread across his face. "I think it is finished . . . I think. And yet something is not . . . is not . . ." His voice drifted off. Shaking his head, he shuffled into the workshop for a little sleep.

Angelo was alone, for the hour was so late that all his

followers had disappeared from the wall. He paid no attention to Nonno's head-shaking doubts but stood silently content, dazzled by the beauty of the fountain and exalted by a feeling of success.

"I shall invite all the cats of Rome to come here at sundown!" he howled into the stillness of dawn. "I will show them the fountain and tell them it is theirs forever and ever!"

On the last note of his triumphant howl, Angelo scaled the tree trunk and sprang over the wall.

NIGHT MEETING
AT THE COURTYARD

SUNSET COLORS STILL brightened the western sky when soft-footed visitors began to arrive in the courtyard. They came singly, in couples, in family groups, and in bands of a dozen or more at a time. Before darkness fell the place was filled with a multitude of cats.

There were venerable cats near the end of their days and kittens whose milky-blue eyes had not long been open. There were sleek, sinewy males, and bulging, sagging females who soon would be mothers. There were black cats and gray ones, yellow cats and white ones, and many with stripes and patches of mixed colors. There were fat cats and lean ones, tough cats and gentle ones, noisy cats, and some who seldom made sounds. Yet all the cats were alike —no one owned them or cared for them and so all of them ran wild in the streets of Rome.

Under Angelo's guidance the cats left a clear area around the fountain and then seated themselves where they could —on the cobblestones, in the plane tree, on top of the rubbish that overflowed from the cans, and up on top of the wall. When Angelo was ready to address his followers he looked out over the courtyard and saw wall-to-wall cats. His heart overflowed with love.

He began by reminding the cats of how and why the fountain had been built. He thanked those in the audience who had helped. Then he pointed out the fairy-like spires, the openwork towers, and the delicate mosaics. His voice became choked with emotion and he called upon Nonno to go on.

Nonno was nervous at first, for he had never before made a speech. But when he looked at the fountain he forgot everything except joy in the thing he had created.

"See this small throne," he said as he touched it lovingly. "Notice its shape, like an open shell. And see the gold around the edges, and the words VIVA ROMA on the back. I made this throne seat for Angelo. When he sits there he will feel the spray on his whiskers. And from here he can dip his paws into the pool and cool them in the water." As Nonno pointed to the pool, a hush fell over the host of cats. The hush was followed by a murmur, which rippled and spread through the crowd.

"Water? What water?" cried a large gray cat who jumped up and sprang to the edge of the fountain. He looked the fountain over with amused contempt and then leaped into the pool. *"What water?"* he repeated in a loud howl. "This fountain is as dry as my tongue on a midsummer day!"

His words traveled through the courtyard, from cat to cat, like a gust of wind through weeds in a vacant lot. Heads bent and nodded as miews grew to meows and meows became howls. Here and there, individual voices rose above the general confusion.

"The fountain is dry!"

"A dry fountain—how do you like that!"

"Angelo and his great plans!"

"What good is a fountain without water?"

Angelo stood on the rim of the empty pool and tried to explain what had happened. But how could he explain when his own disappointment and puzzlement were even greater than theirs?

"We'll get water somehow!" he called out. "Water will shoot upward, over this beautiful tower. And it will fall in a spray into this little pool. It will, I promise you!"

"You and your promises!" said a big yellow cat. "A dry

fountain! And after all the work we did! We've all had our fill of plans and promises."

The yellow cat joined the crowd that was now pushing and shoving its way out through the gate. The cats left faster and more noisily than they had arrived and Angelo was soon alone in the courtyard with Nonno.

"They are right, Nonno," said Angelo sadly. "A fountain without water is no good at all."

Nonno shook his head. "I was afraid we had forgotten something. But anyone can forget things....." His voice drifted off.

"But not *water* for a fountain!" Angelo cried in despair. "Water is the one thing that a fountain must have."

There was a long silence. Then Angelo asked gently, "How does water get into a fountain? Where does the water come from? What makes the water go up first and then down? What makes it fall like a curtain of crystal beads? And how do rainbows get caught in the spray? Tell me, Nonno, please tell me. Then I may think of a plan."

But all Nonno could answer was, "Pipes. It must be the pipes. I try to think and remember, but some things get mixed up in my head."

"Then there is nothing more we can do," said Angelo. "It is my fault more than yours that our fountain is useless."

"But it is still beautiful," said Nonno. "Maybe we can plant some flowers in the pool and..."

"No! No!" Angelo interrupted. "It is a fountain. If it cannot have water, then let it be empty—for now."

Nonno shrugged his shoulders and a great weariness came over him. He took a last look at the airy towers he had built, turned away, and shuffled into the workshop to sleep.

Angelo spent the rest of the night in the plane tree staring down at the dry fountain. He had failed. Even Nonno could no longer help.

A THRONE FOR ANGELO

Summer came again and the days grew hot. Nonno spent less and less time indoors helping Tonio and more and more time behind the tall rubbish cans in the corner of the courtyard, nodding beside the dry fountain.

Angelo, somewhere in the shadows, high on the wall or among the dry dusty leaves of the plane tree, kept a silent watch. By day he stayed by himself in the courtyard, and by night he wandered alone through the streets and alleys of the city. His followers no longer followed but roamed leaderless throughout Rome.

63

Angelo was troubled by this but more deeply troubled by his feelings of personal failure. His followers had believed in him and he had betrayed their trust. For a long time he kept on trying. When he was not on the courtyard wall studying the little fountain, which, in spite of all his wishes, continued to remain dry, he was studying the big fountains in the city piazzas. He observed that each of them had something, usually in the middle, that made water flow upward and then fall gracefully into a pool. But no matter how carefully he watched, he could not discover what it was. He knew only that it was something that was missing from the fountain he and Nonno had made. At last he began to accept his fear that theirs would forever be dry.

One morning Tonio came out of the workshop. "Come in, Nonno," he called. "I have a little work for you to do inside."

Nonno could not hear, or did not wish to hear. He remained hidden in his place in the corner. As Tonio looked around his eye caught glints of color reflected from the fountain's towers.

"What's over there, back of the rubbish?" he called. Then he walked across the courtyard and pushed one of the cans aside. He drew in his breath and stood there with his mouth open as he gazed wordlessly at the bright, shining structure.

"It's a fountain," Nonno said sadly. "I worked on it for a long time, with Angelo. Now it is finished."

"Nonno, it's beautiful!" cried the young workman. "You know, you're quite an artist. It looks a little strange, that thing you made, but it's sort of . . . well, sort of wonderful. But why do you call it a fountain?"

"Because it *is* a fountain!" said Nonno, aware that Angelo was watching and listening from a perch in the tree over his head. "All it needs is water to shoot up here and then fall down—here into this pool."

"Poor, mixed-up Nonno," said Tonio. "Don't you remember how you used to put in big pipes for the fountains my father made? How you used to dig up a whole street, sometimes, to lay the pipes and connect them to the city water? And how we used a pump to keep the water moving?"

Nonno's face lighted up and he spoke eagerly. "Then you can help us get the pipes we need, and the pump and . . ."

Tonio interrupted. "No, no! *Mama mia!* Those things cost a fortune—money, Nonno, much money."

"Then our fountain is no good at all," said Nonno.

Tonio answered kindly, "Yes, it is good. Maybe we can use it for some plants."

"No plants!" cried Nonno, speaking for the first time with authority. "This is a fountain, not a flowerpot!"

"Bravo!" hissed Angelo softly from above.

Tonio shook his head. Then, after staring at the strange bright thing that Nonno had built, he turned and took a good look at the cluttered courtyard. For the first time he felt ashamed of the litter and junk that had accumulated through the years. "I think we should clean up this place," he said to Nonno. "Come on, give me a hand."

For the rest of the day they worked side by side. First they moved all the ugly rubbish cans and bins and put them out of sight behind the building. They used the old pushcart and Nonno hauled load after load of rusty cans and other junk to the nearest dump. Then he pulled weeds that had grown tall and rank, while Tonio trimmed the overgrown geraniums and rose bushes that had long been untended but still clung to life in what had once been a small flower garden.

When it was time for Tonio to go home to his family for the night, the courtyard looked neat and tidy. But layers of dust and grime still lay on the cobblestones, the plants, and the leaves of the old plane tree.

On his way out the gate Tonio stopped and placed his hands on Nonno's shoulders. "See, your pretty little fountain no longer looks so much out of place in our courtyard," he said. "After I leave, get your broom and bucket and see if you can wash away some of this dust."

Nonno was heading for the broom in the workshop when Tonio called him out again. "Wait," said Tonio. "I have a better idea. Use a hose. My father had one around somewhere, years ago. See if you can find it in that big cupboard. And try that old faucet out in back. *Buona notte!"* And Tonio disappeared through the gate.

Nonno found the hose, just where Tonio's old father had left it, neatly coiled, long ago. He dragged it out and fastened one end to the faucet in back of the workshop. He turned on the faucet and, for a moment, no water came. Then there was a strange gurgling, followed by a sudden gush of water from the nozzle of the hose.

Nonno washed off the cobblestones which soon began to shine like pebbles in a tidepool, richly colored in greens, browns, and reds. *"Bella, bella!* This is the way to clean, eh?" he remarked to Angelo.

But the great black cat, near exhaustion from his searches and his worries, was sleeping and dreaming. In his dream he was lying by a fountain and mist from its spray was cooling the air. He awakened with a start. As he opened his eyes he saw his little fountain sparkling through a spray of water.

"Nonno! Nonno!" he cried out in jubilation. "Our fountain works! It's not dry after all! . . . Or am I dreaming?"

"It's no dream," said Nonno with a sad little laugh. "But the only water you see comes from this hose."

The hose was very old and even as Nonno spoke water began to squirt out in all directions through tiny splits and cracks that appeared suddenly in the part just below the nozzle.

"That's it! *That's it!*" cried Angelo as he sprang down from the tree. "Quick, turn off the faucet. And then do just as I say."

Nonno was not entirely sure what Angelo was trying to do. But he followed his directions and worked the nozzle of the hose upward through the beautiful airy towers. Together they adjusted and patched the cracking hose with rag bandages and old tape. They made the hose squirt where Angelo wanted it to squirt—and just before dawn even he was pleased with the effect.

Each time the faucet was turned on water shot upward from the nozzle, which was now slightly visible above the tip of the tallest of the fountain's towers. The water went up, spread out like an open flower, and then cascaded down over and through the openwork of the ornamented towers. At the same time, through the splits and cracks in the hose, fine jets spurted outward in graceful curves. Slowly, the little pool was filling with water.

"So, the fountain is finished," said Nonno.

"Yes, it is finished at last," said Angelo. "We found a way because a way had to be found."

"Do I hear running water?" asked a voice from the top of the wall.

Angelo looked up and saw the yellow cat sitting alone. "Yes, it is water," he answered.

"Then your fountain is not dry after all!" cried the cat as he sprang down and began at once to help himself to a drink from the cool, fresh water.

"Wait!" commanded Angelo. "You will please go at once and tell the others. You will tell them that the Fountain of the Wild Cats will be turned on this evening at sundown. Then all the cats of Rome will be welcome."

That evening, as the sun set over Rome, the back streets

and alleyways of the city seemed strangely empty of cats. However, any Romans wandering in the vicinity of the Fabrica Di Fontane would have seen a strange sight. From all directions they came—tough cats and gentle cats, big cats and small cats, old gray-whiskered cats and cuddly young kittens, lean young hunters and expectant mothers. Over the wall of the little courtyard they went, all of them headed for the fountain where water spurted and sparkled in the evening light.

On the rim of the little pool in the Viva Roma throne was Angelo, one paw held in the cooling water. If ever a cat could be said to smile, then Angelo was smiling.